This book belongs to

....

....

Written by Ronne Randall
Illustrated by Tony Kerins

First published 2008 by Parragon Books, Ltd.

5005 Newport Drive, Rolling Meadows, Illinois 60008

10 9 8 7 6 5 4 3 2 1

ISBN 978-1-68052-537-3

Parragon Books is an imprint of Cottage Door Press, LLC.

Before I go to sleep

Parragon

Before I go to sleep,
Mommy brings my drink,
and kisses me
night-night.

Night-night,
Mommy.

Daddy reads me a story
about the little red sailboat.

Then he kisses me
night-night.

Night-night,
Daddy.

Where is Waggy dog?

There you are.
Night-night, Waggy dog.

Before I go to sleep,
I kiss Teddy bear night-night.

Night-night, Teddy bear.
Are you sleepy yet?

Kitty isn't sleepy yet.

I wonder where
she goes at night?

Before I go to sleep,
I'll snuggle down,
and close my eyes.

Where is Teddy bear going?
Teddy bear and Waggy dog
are following Kitty.
Wait for me, I'll come *too.*

We'll sail away in our
little red sailboat

over Grandma and Grandpa's house

and across the pond to say,

Night-night, ducks. Night-night, sky.

Night-night, moon.

Night-night, stars,

Night-night, world.

Teddy bear, are you sleepy yet?
We're almost home, now.

Night-night, me.

Night-night, you.

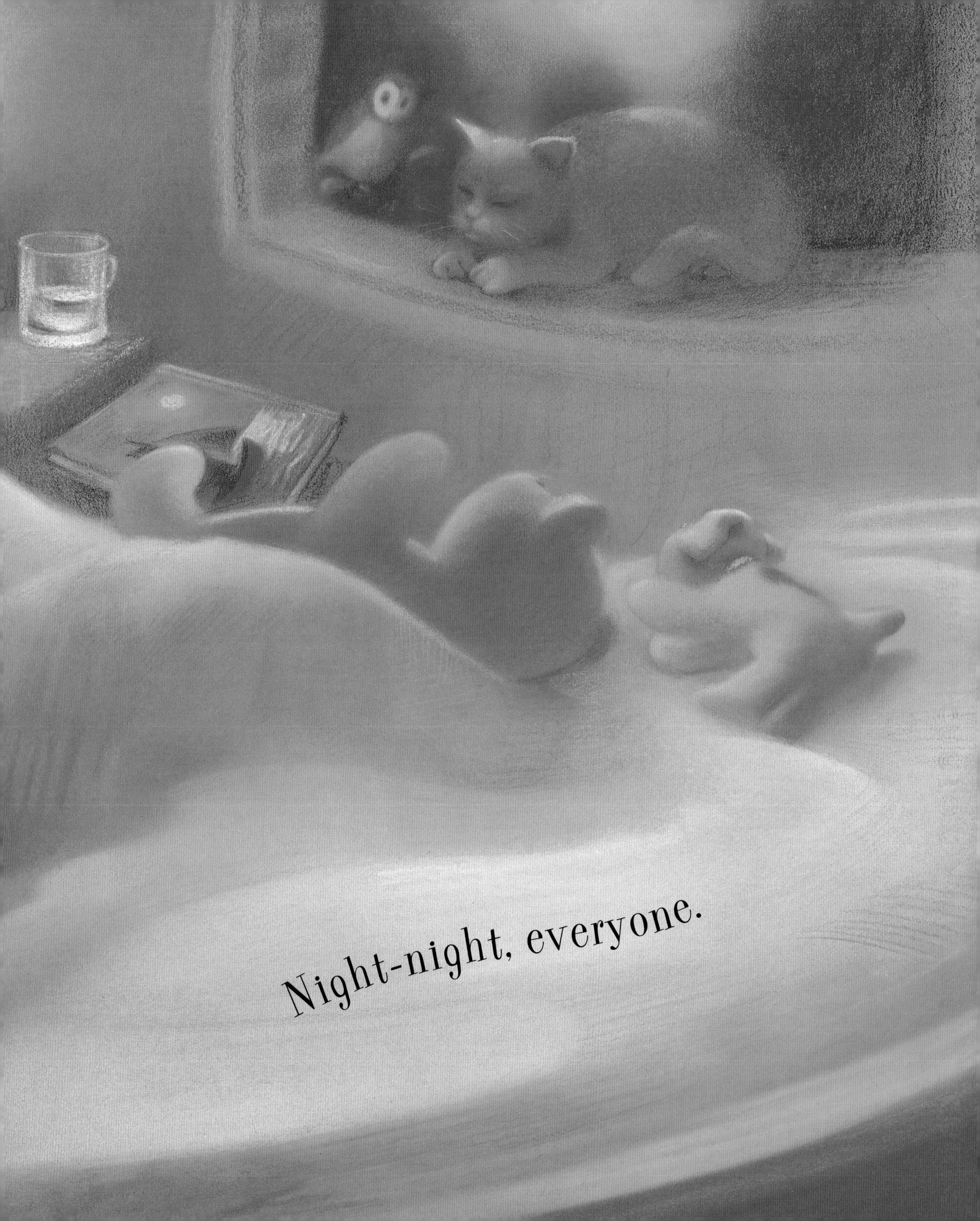
Night-night, everyone.

Sweet dreams